Other books by Mick Inkpen:

KIPPER
KIPPER'S TOYBOX
KIPPER'S BIRTHDAY
KIPPER'S BOOK OF COLOUR
KIPPER'S BOOK OF COUNTING
KIPPER'S BOOK OF OPPOSITES
ONE BEAR AT BEDTIME
THE BLUE BALLOON
THREADBEAR
BILLY'S BEETLE
PENGUIN SMALL
LULLABYHULLABALLOO!

British Library Cataloguing in Publication Data

A catalogue record for this book is available
from the British Library

ISBN 0 340 59850 6

First published 1994
10 9 8 7 6 5 4 3 2 1

Published by Hodder and Stoughton Children's Books,
a division of Hodder Headline plc,
47 Bedford Square, London WC1B 3DP

Printed in Italy by L.E.G.O., Vicenza

KIPPER'S BOOK OF
WEATHER
Mick Inkpen

HODDER AND STOUGHTON
London   Sydney   Auckland

Rain

Sunshine

Snow

Ice

Fog

Wind

Hailstones

Rainbow!